SpongeBob's Best Days!

A GOLDEN BOOK • NEW YORK

Created by

Stephen Hillenburg

ISBN: 978-0-375-84100-2

www.randomhouse.com/kids

Printed in the United States of America

12 11 10

It's Squidward's favorite time of the day—clarinet practice.

Squidward's neighbors have called a vet because they thought there was a sick animal in his house.

Squilliam Fancyson, an old enemy from band class, calls Squidward.

Squilliam tells Squidward he's now the leader of a big fancy band.

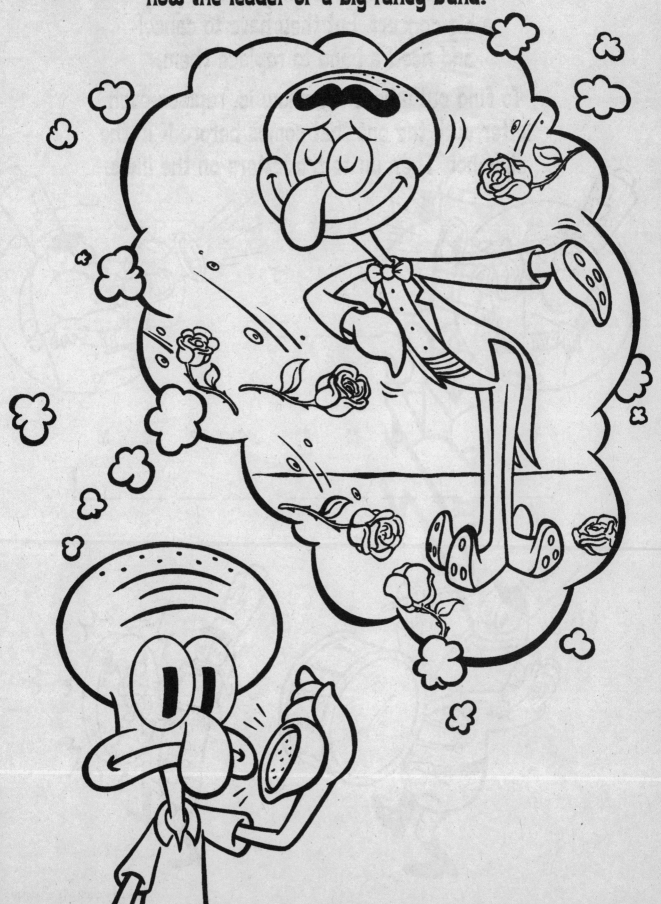

Really Big Show!

Squilliam's band is supposed to play
a big concert, but they have to cancel
and need a band to replace them.

To find out where the show is, replace each
letter with the one that comes before it in the
alphabet. Then write the letters on the lines.

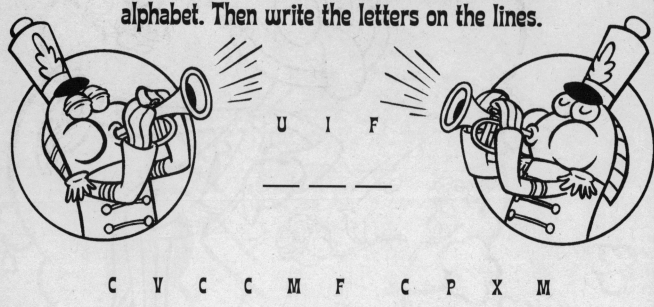

U I F

___ ___ ___

C V C C M F   C P X M

___ ___ ___ ___ ___ ___   ___ ___ ___ ___ !

Squidward says his band will play the big show!

But now he has to find a band!

It's Instrumental!

(A game for two players)

To help Squidward find instruments for his band, take turns with a friend connecting the dots below.

If you make a square, give yourself 1 point.
A 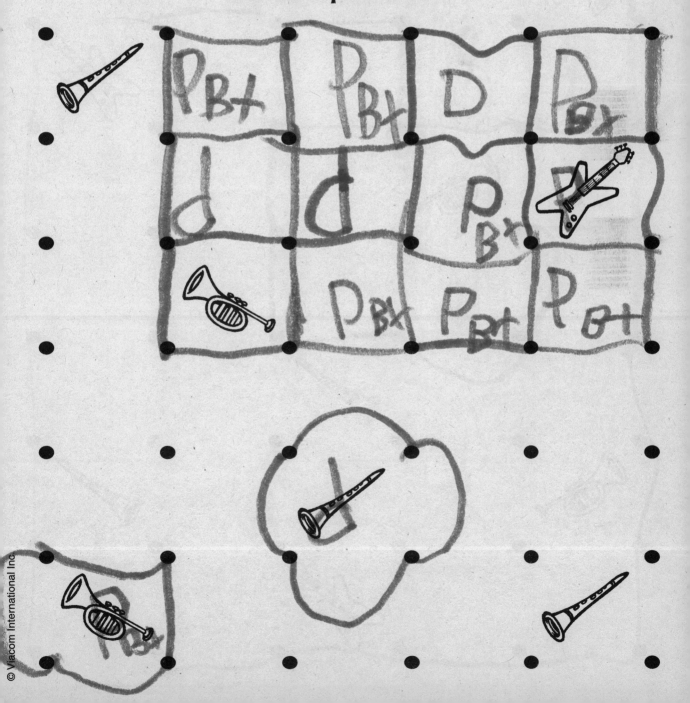 or a within a square is worth 2 points.
A is worth 4 points.
When no more squares can be made, the player with more points wins.

Play again!

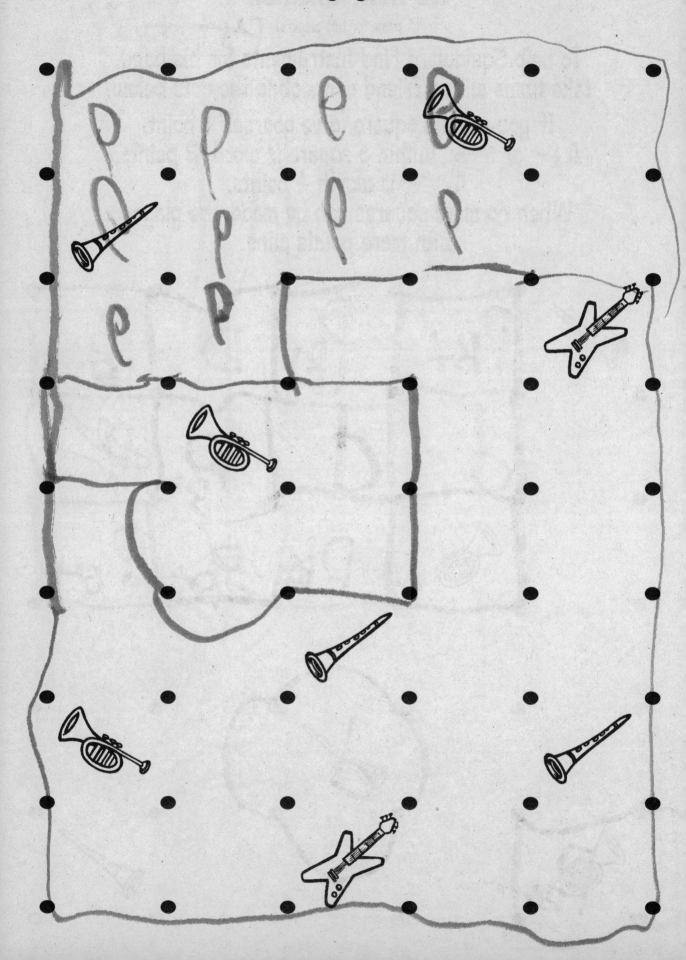

Everyone in Bikini Bottom gets excited about joining the band.

Patrick and SpongeBob are ready for band practice.

"How many of you have played musical
instruments before?" Squidward asks.

"Is mayonnaise an instrument?"

"Errr . . . no," says Squidward.
"Don't worry, I have enough talent for all of you."

Band practice doesn't go very well.

"I have an idea! People talk loudly when
they want to sound smart, right?"

"THAT'S CORRECT!"

"So maybe if we play really loudly," says Squidward,
"people might think we're good."

SpongeBob pumps up the noise.

"I have a new idea," Squidward says.
"Maybe we should play so quietly no one can hear us."

"Maybe we wouldn't sound so bad if some people weren't playing with big meaty claws!"

"Bring it on! BRING IT ON!"

"No, people, let's be smart and bring it off."

"Oh, now the talking cheese is going to tell us what to do!"

SpongeBob and Patrick try to keep the peace with music . . .

. . . but it doesn't work.

Band practice hits all the wrong notes.

"Look at the time," says Sandy. "Band practice is over. Buh-bye."

"You took my one true chance for happiness and crunched it into little, bite-sized pieces," says Squidward. "Thanks for nothing."

"You're welcome!"

"We're monsters," says SpongeBob. "We've failed him."

"Squidward's always been there for us when it was easy for him!"

"Larry," says SpongeBob. "When you got sick from eating all those tanning pills, who was there to help you?"

"A fireman," says Larry.

"Right!" says SpongeBob. "If we could all pretend that Squidward was a fireman, I'm sure we could all pull together! Let's make Squidward proud."

The most important part of being in a band
is looking the part, so everybody practices hard.

The band heads out for a practice concert at the Clam Dancer, Bikini Bottom's loudest rock club.

SpongeBob lets the rock roll!

. . . SpongeBob surfs the crowd.

After the show, Patrick says, "Being on tour makes me feel wild. Let's wreck this hotel room!"

"Patrick, this isn't a hotel. It's my house."

Being a superstar for a night is wearing SpongeBob down!

"The music is stale, SpongeBob. I need to go solo."

SpongeBob convinces Patrick to stay.
"You're right, we do need a new
sound and a new look for the Bubble Bowl."

The band decides to wear marching uniforms.
Captain SpongeBob's Jellyfish Jam Band
is ready for the Bubble Bowl!

The Big Time

It's the day of the big show!
Help Squidward get to the Bubble Bowl.

Start

Finish

Squidward doesn't think his band is coming.

"Hi," says Squilliam. "I had to be here to watch you blow your big chance. Where's your band?"

"We're right here," says SpongeBob.

"And we're ready to play!"

"Okay, everybody, let's get this over with."

SpongeBob kicks off the show.

Hitting the High Notes

To find out what Squidward says about his band when he hears them, begin at START and write each letter in order in the blanks below.

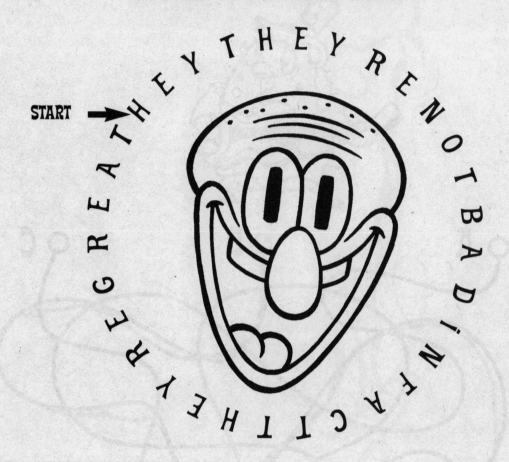

START → THEY THEY RENOTBADINFACTHEYREGREAT

"<u>Hey, they're not</u>
<u>bad! in fact,</u>
<u>they're Great</u>!"

Amped Up!

Help Mrs. Puff find the line that will plug into her amplifier so she can play her solo.

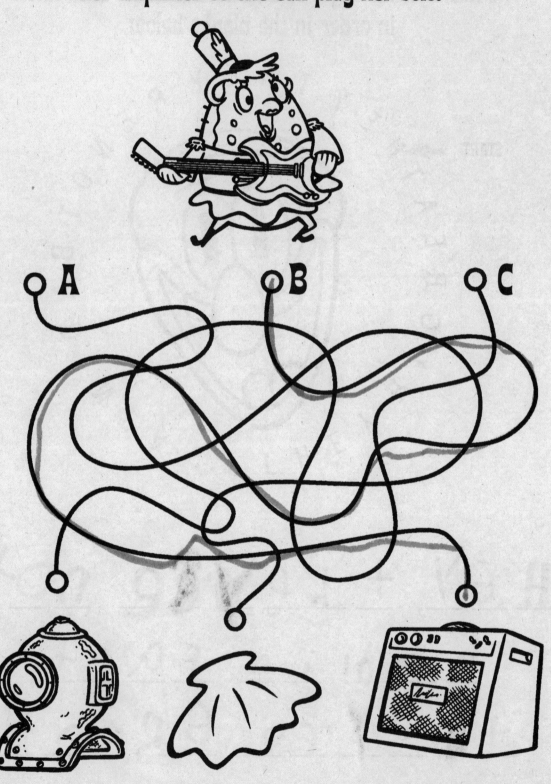

Mrs. Puff lets it rip!

Time for the big finish . . .

. . . and the big light show!

I'm Ready . . . to Rock!
Help SpongeBob finish his new song by filling in the blanks.

I've got a song in my

_____ ,

and I'm ready to play my

_____ .

Music makes me _____

like a jellyfish.

To _____ and _____

is my wish!

I'm ready to rock!

I wanna _____ and scream!

Jump and _____ !

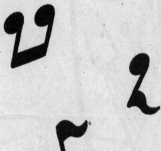

Let's rap, let's roll, let's _____ march _____ all day.

I'm gonna paint my _____ strings _____

and wear electric _____ Gittars _____!

My boots are taller than two ~~shoes~~ _____ ,

and my pants are made of _____ Leater _____ !

I'm ready to rock!

Squilliam's world has been rocked!

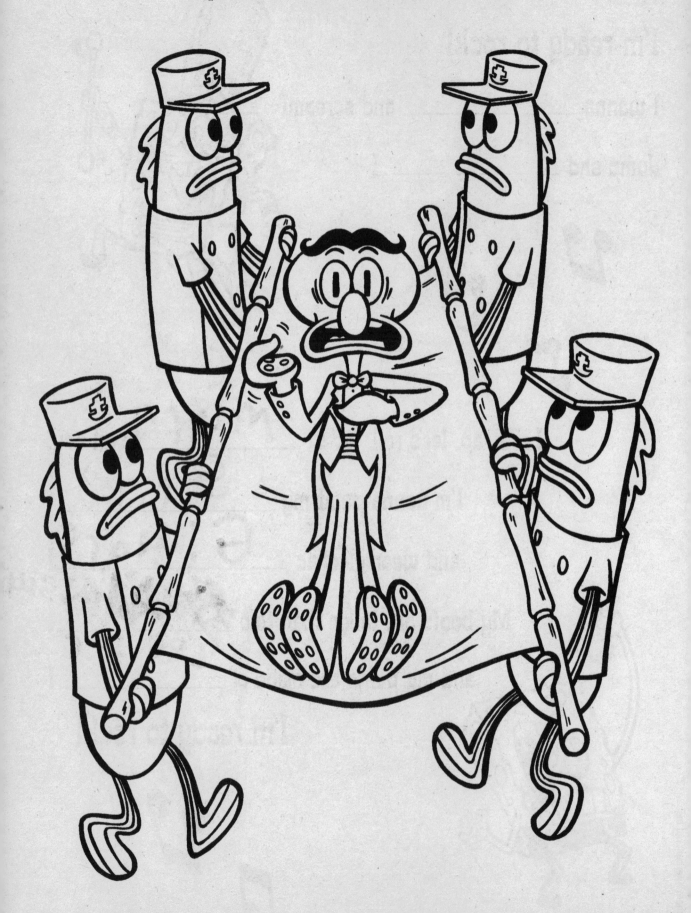

This could be the greatest day of Squidward's life!

But the next day, Squidward has changed his mind about SpongeBob's new love of music.

Fly Like a Fish

The proud jellyfish hunter is quietly getting ready . . .

Jellyfish jam!
How many jellyfish can you spot?

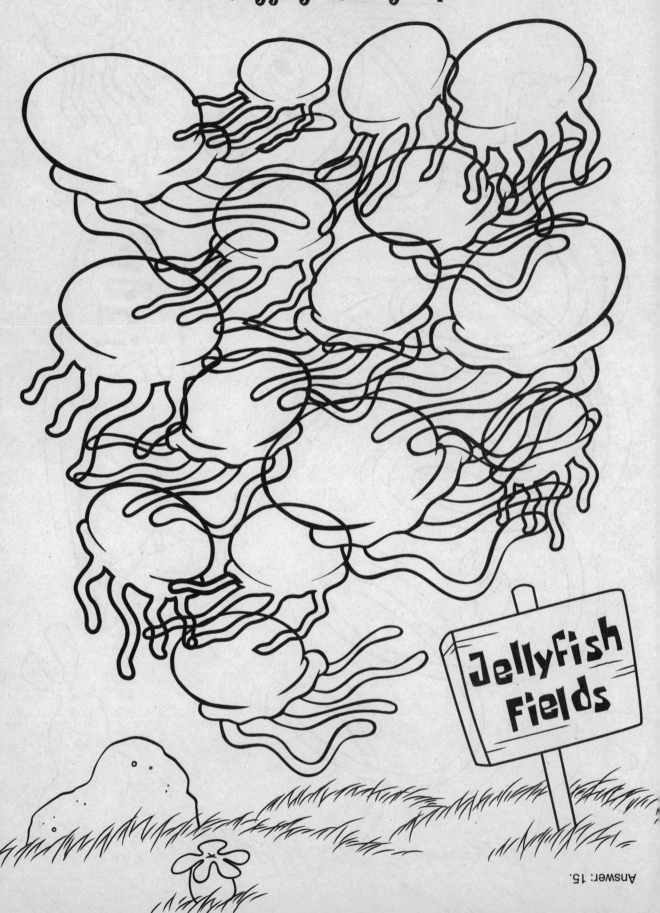

Answer: 15.

A bounce too far.

SpongeBob remembers his grandfather's words:
"If we were meant to fly, we'd have propellers on our heads!"

"Look, Patrick! I've built my very own flying machine!"

"Landing gear: check! Complimentary peanuts: check!
IGNITION!"

"Patrick, when you pedal, I'll be pulled into the sky. It has to work!"

"Maybe my dream of flying with the jellyfish isn't meant to be."

"Look, Gary! I was just trying to dry off and now I'm floating!"

"Help! Won't someone save my snail?"

Oh, no! Mr. Krabs's dime is trapped on the roof of the Krusty Krab! Help SpongeBob find the right path to get it.

A   B   C

10¢

"Oh, help! Won't someone please clean my tub?"

"I've got to give these feverish favor-seekers the slip."

"Hey, he's getting away! He owes us favors!"

SpongeBob's neighbors are driving him crazy! Help him fly away.

START

FINISH

Suddenly, a daredevil with a cannon pops SpongeBob's pants!

"Look what we've done . . . to those wonderful pants!"

"I guess it was fun while it lasted—huh?"

"Hey, if you want to fly, all you need are friends!
Thanks, jellyfish!"

"No more flying on my own, Patrick.
I'll leave that to the jellyfish."

"Suit yourself, SpongeBob!"

Don't Pencil Me In!

One day, while SpongeBob and Patrick
are blowing bubbles . . .

"It's a giant pencil! Let's draw some giant pictures!"

"Your work's not very realistic, SpongeBob."

"SpongeBob! Your pictures are coming to life!"

"Now, that's more like it, Mr. Critic!"

"Now All I Need Is a Magic Mustache!"

Copy the smaller picture into the larger boxes and make Patrick's dream come true!

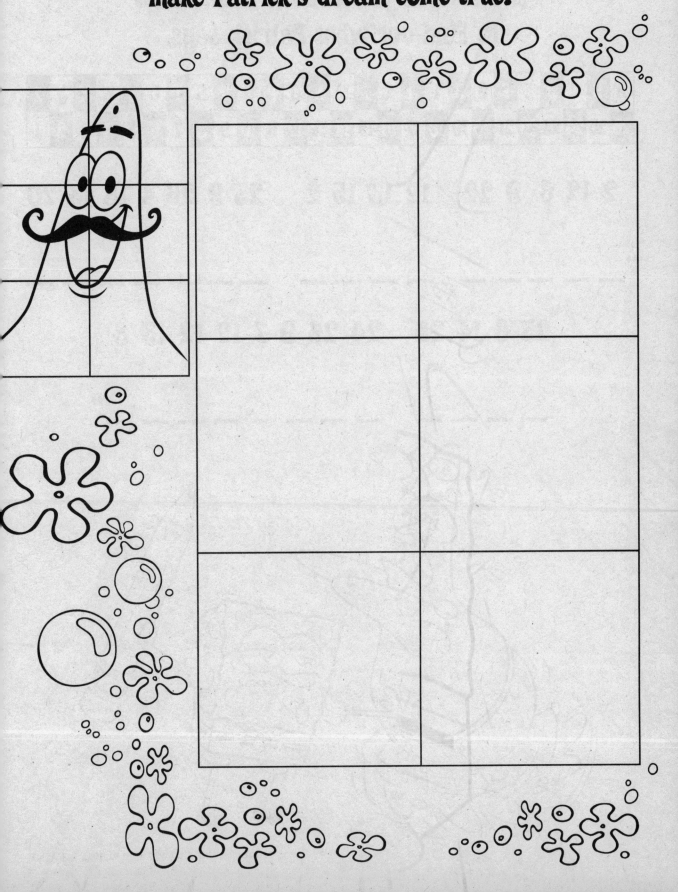

Pencil Power!

SpongeBob tells Patrick that being an artist is a serious job. Use the code below to find out what Patrick says.

A	B	C	D	E	F	G	H	I	J	K	L	M	N	O	P	Q	R	S	T	U	V	W	X	Y	Z
26	25	24	23	22	21	20	19	18	17	16	15	14	13	12	11	10	9	8	7	6	5	4	3	2	1

2 12 6 9 22   12 13 15 2   23 9 26 4 18 13 20

"____ ____, _____

23 6 14 25   24 26 9 7 12 12 13 8

_____ _____"

SpongeBob decides to play a prank on Squidward.
"I'll draw a picture of me . . ."

"...and the picture will knock on
Squidward's door. Then ...."

"Oh, no!"

DoodleBob has escaped with the Magic Pencil. Help SpongeBob and Patrick get through the maze to catch up to him.

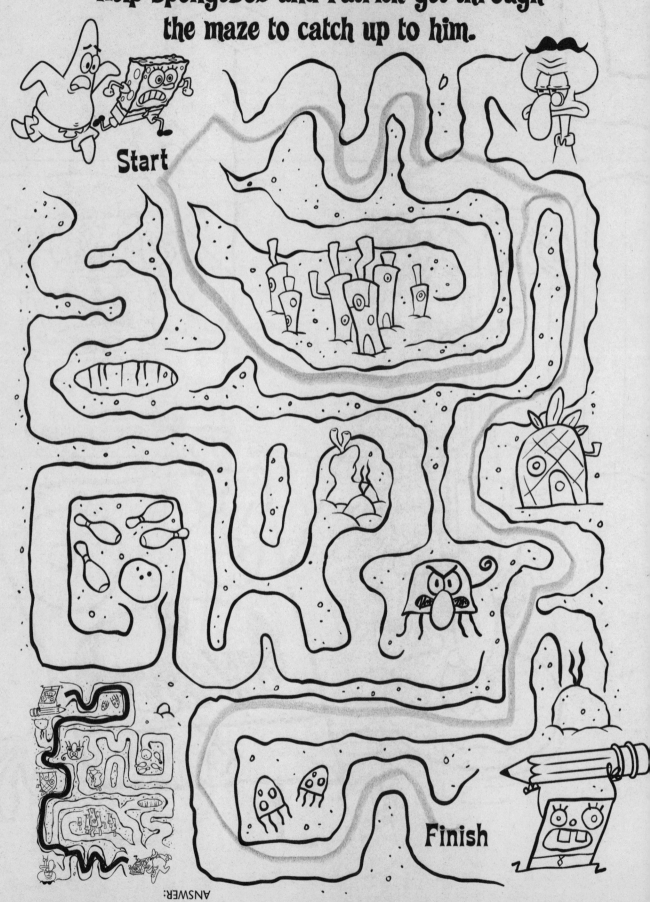

Start

Finish

"SpongeBob, that doodle is horrible . . .
the bulgy eyes . . . the buckteeth . . . the stupid tie!"

DoodleBob draws a bowling ball and bowls Patrick over!

SpongeBob grabs the pencil and starts erasing DoodleBob!

You Missed a Spot!

SpongeBob thinks he erased the troublemaking DoodleBob, but he didn't get all of him. To find out what SpongeBob left behind, replace each letter with the one that comes before it in the alphabet.

E P P E M F C P C T   M F G U   B S N

_ _ _ _ _ _ _ _ _ ' _   _ _ _ _   _ _ _ !

Later that night, SpongeBob does a little decorating.

"Good night, Magic Pencil."

DoodleBob sneaks in during the night and redraws the rest of his body. Now he's after SpongeBob!

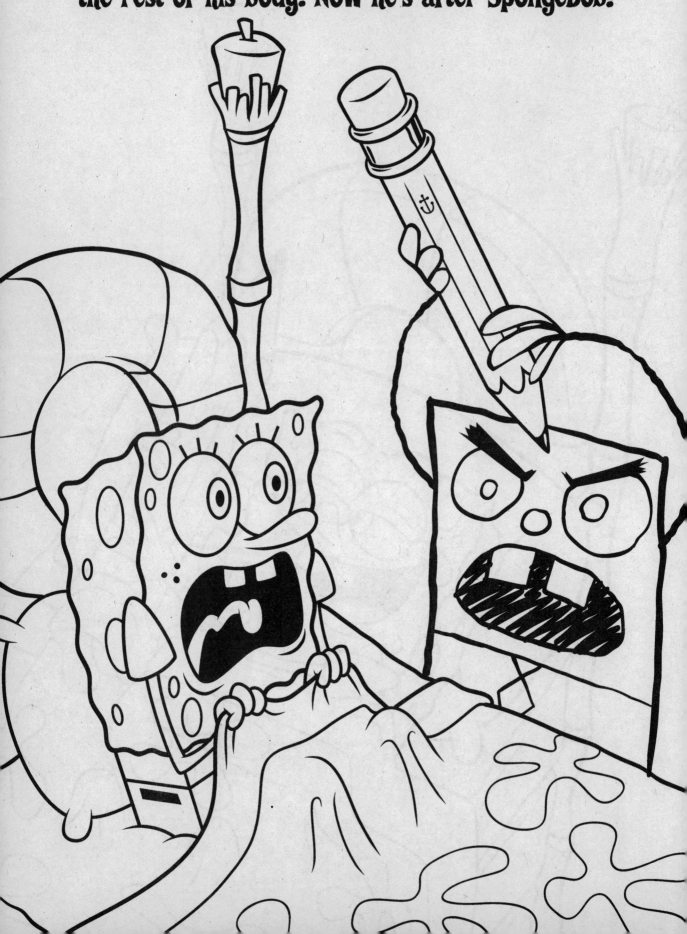

"It looks like a draw!"

DoodleBob grabs the eraser
and uses it to rub out SpongeBob.

SpongeBob quickly redraws himself.

DoodleBob steps onto a piece of paper and is trapped!

Page for Mr. Doodle!

"Yikes! That evil doodle is on your wall, SpongeBob!"

"No, he wasn't evil. He was merely a simple drawing stuck in our aquatic world."

"Magic Pencil, your power is too mighty. I will send you back to your kingdom."

Good-bye, Magic Pencil!

Picture Perfect
Make a doodle of yourself.
(Be careful. Don't let it escape!)

Friends Forever?

"Happy Valentine's Day, Bikini Bottom!"

Funny Little Valentines

- Use your crayons or markers to decorate both sides of the cards below.

- Have a grown-up help you cut them out.

- Give them to your best mates!

To _____

From _____

You're My Treasure!

From _____

"Happy Valentine's Day, SpongeBob. I'm nuts for you!"

"I'm bubbles for you, Sandy."

"Patrick's going to love the giant chocolate balloon
you made for him, SpongeBob."

"Here's the plan: Patrick and I will ride the Ferris wheel at the Valentine's Day carnival . . ."

"... then you arrive in the balloon for maximum visual impact!"

"Oh, Patrick! Do you want the greatest, bestest, most fantabulous Valentine's Day surprise ever?"

"Please, please, tell me what it is. Ruin the surprise!
I HAVE TO KNOW!"

"Patrick, maybe you should look on top of Mount Climb-Up-and-Fall-Off."

"I don't see it."

"Oh, no! A pack of chocolate-eating scallops are trying
to rassle up this balloon!"

Can you help SpongeBob get Patrick to the Valentine's Day Carnival?

"Wow, you got me my own carnival! Hey, everybody, get out of my carnival!"

"Don't be silly, Patrick. The whole fair isn't yours."

Unscramble these letters to see what other things Patrick thinks SpongeBob got for him.

O N O T T C   D N A Y C

_____   _____

O T H   O D G   N D A S T

___   ___   _____

R E R Y M - O G - D N U R O

_____ - __ - _____

E R H E T   K H A S S R

_____   _____

"Just keep looking out there, pal, and you'll see your gift.
Come in, Sandy. It's showtime!"

"Errr, you know how sometimes things don't . . . ummm . . . work out? Well, here's your gift—a big, friendly handshake!"

"Oh, boy! We're having fun now, Patrick!"

Decorate the roller coaster car.

"I've been thinking, SpongeBob. A handshake doesn't seem like much, but I guess it's the thought that counts."

"Oh, hi, SpongeBob. We want to thank you for the gifts.
I can't believe we only met today and you gave me a bike!"

"Patrick needs love, too!"

"Yahoo! Git along, little shellfish!"

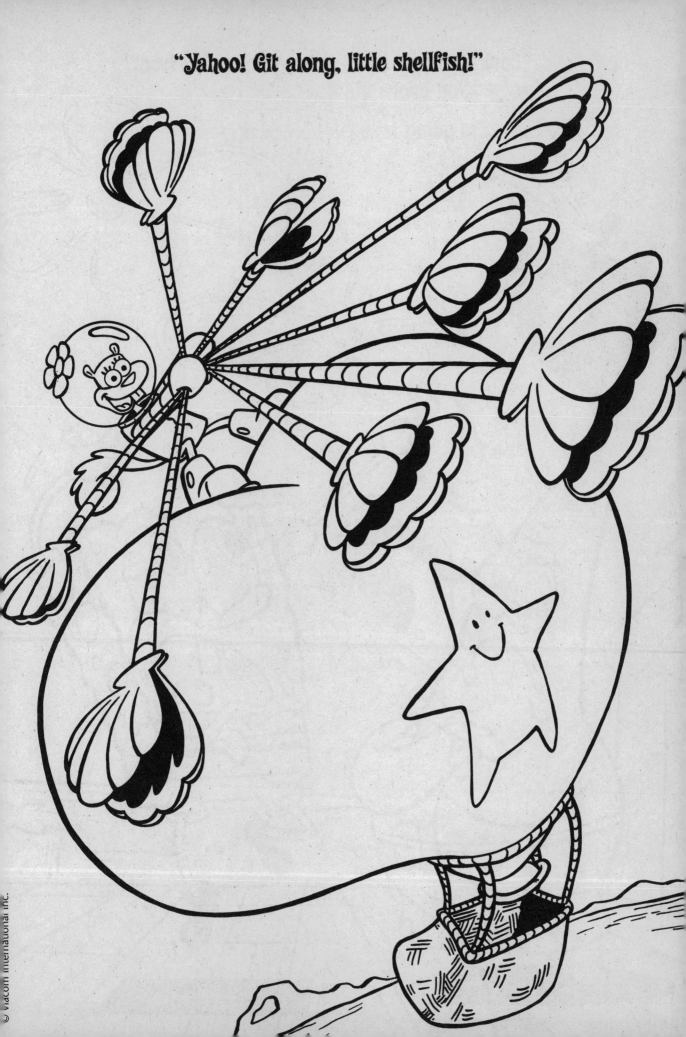

"Patrick, no! The balloon will . . ."

Shiver Me Timbers!

"Can't you see the sign? Go away!"

"I guess he doesn't want our money. Let's go someplace else."

"You mean if we stayed open at night, you'd give us your money?"

"Welcome to the night shift, boys! I have to go, since I have a life."

"I'm swabbing the bathroom . . . at night!"

"I'll do it for the Krusty Krab! Aaaaaaiiiiiyyyyyy!"

Help SpongeBob get back to the Krusty Krab...FAST!

START

FINISH

ANSWER:

"Who's the Hash-Stinging...Sash-Bringing...Mash-Winging...?"

"The Hash-Slinging Slasher is the ghost of a fry cook who died right here! He has a spatula for a hand!"

There are three warning signs that the Hash-Slinging Slasher is coming. (They're secret, so you'll need this key to decode them.)

A	B	C	D	E	F	G	H	I	J	K	L	M	N	O	P	Q	R	S	T	U	V	W	X	Y	Z
26	25	24	23	22	21	20	19	18	17	16	15	14	13	12	11	10	9	8	7	6	5	4	3	2	1

1. the lights go
   7 19 22   15 18 20 19 7 8   20 12

   off and on!
   12 21 21   26 13 23   12 13

2. the Phone rings!
   7 19 22   11 19 12 13 22   9 18 13 20 8

3. his ghostly bus
   19 18 8   20 19 12 8 7 15 2   25 6 8

   arrives!
   26 9 9 18 5 22 8

Draw what you think the Hash-Slinging Slasher might look like.

"Ha ha! I made the whole thing up, SpongeBob."

"This is silly, SpongeBob! No one in his right mind wants a Krabby Patty at three in the morning!"

"Mmmmm, it's snack time!"

"There's no time to play with the lights when I have a whole ceiling to mop!"

Ring! Ring!
Gulp! "There's no one there, SpongeBob!"

"You're so thoughtful, going to all this trouble to scare me, Squidward."

"This is really happening, SpongeBob!
Look! The walls are dripping green slime!
Wait—they always do that."

SOMETHING'S REALLY WRONG HERE!
Can you find the Squidward who doesn't match?

ANSWER: D.

"Squidward, I didn't know the buses ran this late."

"The buses don't run this late, SpongeBob. It's...it's..."

"He's stepping out of the shadows, SpongeBob. He's...HE'S..."

"Hi. I'd like a job, please. I brought my own spatula."

You
SNOOZE,
You LOSE

"What's the big rush to get your chores done, Sandy?"

"I start hibernating next week. That means
I'll be asleep all winter! There's so much to do first!"

"But Sandy...that means
we only have 168 hours of playtime left!"

"We gotta climb things! We gotta jump off stuff! We gotta ride!"

One day with Sandy has worn out SpongeBob!
Cut out the pieces and tape him back together in order.
When you're finished, color the picture.
(Hint: Tape the pieces on the back.
This will make it easier to color.)

"C'mon, SpongeBob, there's no time to rest!
I'm going to do that all winter!"

"I'm impressed with you, SpongeBob.
You're making this the best pre-hibernation week ever!"

"Gee, a tandem ride through the park sounds safe ... err ... I mean fun!"

The real action is at the industrial park! Can you help SpongeBob and Sandy find their way through?

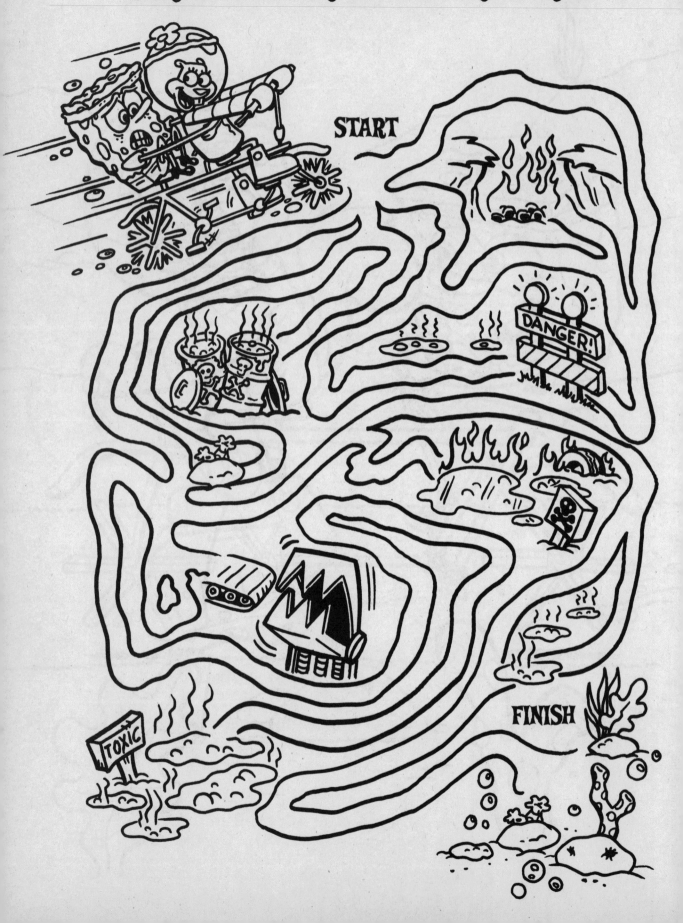

"Now it's time for a down-home favorite...
find the hay in the needle stack! SpongeBob?"

"I've got to leave before that squirrel kills me!
I know, I'll hide under Patrick's rock!"

"That's funny ... SpongeBob always folds his clothes
before running around nude!
Something terrible must have happened to him!"

"Listen up, y'all . . . SpongeBob's gone missing!
I'm rounding up a search party."

"Keep looking! Put your dorsal fins into it! Check the sulfur fields! Don't forget to check that moist cave!"

"How about a break? We've been at this for days!"

"Oh, look, SpongeBob is over there in the sky."

"Hey, where'd everybody go?"

"She'll never find us under this rock.
Wait a minute . . . is that SpongeBob?"

"Oh, look! It is I, SpongeBob, out here in the open!"

"C'mon, SpongeBob, there's still time to go atom smashing!"

"Thank Neptune for hibernation."

Where Is Everybody?
(A memory game for one or two players.)

1. Color the cards on the next four pages,
then cut them out along the dotted lines.

2. Shuffle the cards, then lay them out facedown.

3. Players take turns flipping over two cards at a time.
If the cards match, the player keeps them. If they don't match,
the cards should be put back where they were, facedown.

4. Whoever has more pairs
when all of the cards are picked wins!